DEAD THE LONG YEAR

JUSTIN P. HOPPER

Copyright © 2025 Justin P. Hopper

Published Exclusively and Globally by Far West Press

All rights reserved. No part of this book may be reproduced in any form or by any electronic or mechanical means, including information storage and retrieval systems, without written permission from the publisher or author, except in the case of a reviewer, who may quote brief passages in a review. Scanning, uploading, and electronic distribution of this book or the facilitation of such without the permission of the publisher is prohibited. Your support of the author's rights is appreciated.

This is a work of fiction. All names, characters, businesses, places, events, and incidents are either the products of the author's imagination or used in a fictitious manner. Any resemblance to actual persons, living or dead, or actual events is purely coincidental.

www.farwestpress.com

First Edition

ISBN 979-8-9913506-8-6

Printed in the United States of America

Cover Artwork by Spencer Gore (1878-1914). Study for a Mural Decoration for 'The Cave of the Golden Calf'. Courtesy of Tate Images

Inside illustrations by Tom Eglington

DRAMATIS PERSONAE

1912:
Joan Hayes / Jeanne Eugenie Heyse / Ione de Forest ... An actress, artist and dancer.

Victor B. Neuburg ... A poet and occultist.

Nina Hamnett ... An artist.

Wilfred Merton ... An engraver, publisher and book collector.

Eugene 'Bunko' Wieland ... A publisher.

William Edward 'Teddy' Hayter Preston ... A writer.

Mona Limerick ... An actress.

Arthur Machen ... A writer and actor.

Frida Uhl ... A nightclub founder.

Aleister Crowley ... A practitioner of magick.

Anne Bradley ... A tragic young woman.

2023:
Justin Hopper ... A psychogeographer, of sorts.

In memory of Jeanne Heyse, a remarkable young woman.

With special thanks to Caroline Neuburg.

For Lucy.

We can begin, as is tradition in such cases, with a gun in the hand of an actress. But Chekhov never imagined a gun of such beauty as this. Hammerless, American-made, a handle plated in mother-of-pearl and inlaid with a sunburst. William Morris would have approved of the design and of the thing itself; both useful and beautiful – a shot into the heart of all who viewed it.

So, too, the actress. Useful and beautiful. But, therein lay the problem. To some she was useful as a chip or a notch, something for barter or banter. There was no doubting her beauty by any who saw her. She danced, or not even – just stepped onto the stage – and hearts began to burst from chests. And for a while that had been enough. But her usefulness made it tough.

A man, one of several men who wished they could – poets, all, of course – had read poetry to her recently. They were *always* reading poetry to her, and while she loved poetry, she was far more ambivalent about having men read it to her. It always seemed accompanied by the same choreography of a hand slipping up her thigh. And while she paid attention to the poems themselves, to the words, the men seemed not to care about them, directing their attention to the hand, and to the slipping.

At least this time it was *him*, and it wasn't one of *his* poems. She loved his poems, as she loved him, but there were *so many of them*. This time it was the Italian's — the only one who mattered — and amounted to a lament for the wings of Icarus, their feathers and wax drifting in the sea, damned to drift forever. And a phrase had stood out to her: 'sways like pale wreckage'.

Yes, she thought. That's it.

Pale wreckage.

'Ruined in the eddies alone.'

Joan pointed out that line as Her Poet read; stopped him and made him read it again. He noticed it too, this time, listened to the words as he read them.

'Pale wreckage.'

'The eddies, alone.'

'Glorious,' said Victor. 'He's the King, isn't he, D'Annunzio? And you and I, his prince and princess; or maybe his queens?'

She had to snicker. At least he had a sense of humour about himself.

'He's written a play that's on at the Cave Wednesday – we'll go.'

There was a brief pause. He repeated, but as a question.

'We'll go?'

It was his modern way, this asking. He wanted to simply tell her what to do but was trying his best not to. He was a good one. And she would go, of course. The Cave was one of the eddies — one of *her* eddies — and it required its wreckage, which she felt obliged to offer.

They were all Cave-dwellers in one way or another. For their friends, 'The Cave' was the late-night hostelry they all gathered in. Joan had a far more private cave of her own, though it was less glamorous. Hers was the one she inhabited – the studio in which she painted, a single room with light as soon as the sun rose and darkness once it set. Yes, it was where she painted, and that's what she told people. The reality was more like this: she lived in it, and there were paints.

Joan had a habit of rearranging her surroundings while thinking, and she was deep in thought – but there were so few things to move around her temporary home; more a 'hotel', albeit one in which she felt a novel kind of safety. At her father's house in Brixton, and it was certainly *her father's house* and never 'her home', Joan had always been second or third in line behind her sisters, and they second or third in line behind the boarders that paid their way. At her husband's flat in Cardinal Mansions, and it was certainly *her husband's flat* and never 'her home', she'd always been second or third in line behind a stack of books and drawings that seemed fantastically dull if, no doubt, dryly comforting – no colours, no vibrations, no magick, just the same stories again and again, his thrill coming from an unusual binding or a famous provenance.

Earlier that summer, Joan had left London for the first time. She and Victor had gone to France, where they stayed at what – for their budget – was a glamorous eddy; the Hôtel des Écoles in Paris, where they had paused their rampant infidelity a few times, just long enough to visit art galleries, coffee houses and tourist sites. (It was difficult for Joan to see it as *infidelity* of course, as she'd been with Victor since long before marrying her husband. They had continued during the courtship and throughout the wedding period, and ever since as well. It was a constant, whereas the marriage was an eddy swirled up by others – through ceaseless shaking and meddling – and largely against her will.)

In Paris, Victor had – for one day – travelled across the whole of the city meeting with friends-of-friends who might, he mistakenly believed, publish his work. She spent that day around the hotel's neighbourhood, strolling Paris parks, speaking her two or three sentences of French. It was, she recognised by lunchtime, the longest she'd spent comfortably alone since childhood. She was often lonely, but almost never alone. It was the greatest moment of her time abroad; greater still than the 'lustful and damnable promenade of shames' she and he had performed, as her husband had later put it. He'd said repeatedly it would all end in dread, and he was certainly correct on both counts. But to what end was it, this being so often *right*?

Those hours in Paris, unknown and unwatched and unremarkable, had changed everything. It had brought her solace and mischief; and a new dress. And a gun.

Their hotel was in what the couple called the Poetry District, and near to the cemetery – not an accident; Victor insisted on being as close to Baudelaire as possible, 'that our souls, alas, be bold enough!' – and while boldness was a hot commodity in the area, such freshness suited their tastes, particularly Joan's. (Immediately upon return to London, Joan made plans with Nina to go back and remain for good.) The boundaries of the cemetery provided ample space for the kinds of salesmen who required room to run should the constables come, and it was there they had found so many of their souvenirs. In a particularly Dionysian fit on her solo jaunt, Joan purchased for herself the truest gift she had ever had, the revolver – as an *objet d'art* rather than a weapon, of course.

Her dress, too, was from Paris. Her new favourite dress; perhaps the truest dress she had ever worn. Not bought there but, rather, seen on the form of a beautiful woman 20 years Joan's elder, mesmerising her way through the streets of Montparnasse. Joan followed her for as far as her legs could stretch, trying to work up the nerve – and the French – to say *anything* to her, but neither gall nor Gallic phrase arrived, and she had to make do with a thousand memories of every stitch woven into a fast jumble of a mental portrait to pass on to her patient dressmaker back in London. The resulting copy was divine, and bizarre; a Euclidean riot of colours and shapes that combined into something akin to camouflage – so visceral, so *abondante* and *abandonnée* as to be invisible, the desired final state.

And here she was now, mere weeks later, pulling the dress over her head and slipping the revolver and a London map into a fold of material she'd sewn into it for this very purpose, its patches of incoherence defying any sign of the deadly bump tucked beneath.

The dress was her armour, the pistol her sword, the knight prepared to venture from her cave to *The* Cave.

First, however, she must complete her compulsive rearrangement of the studio. Unable to stay with her husband, Wilfred, and unwilling to move in with Victor, she had snatched up a few belongings during one final row and fled to the studio. Only the most important possessions had made the journey: a small writing desk, borne on the back of a strong passer-by whose labour she won with a flutter of eyelashes. Nina's sketch of circus acrobats balanced on top of one another, all on a rickety stack of tables and chairs, the entire sculptural mess of humanity teetering. Wreckage-to-be. Nina meant for it to become a painting but, as she told Joan, 'we're *artists* – who among us has time to *paint*?' A bottle of absinthe she'd brought for Wilfred from Paris – one of the half-dozen-thousand-or-so straws that broke that camel's back. (In hindsight, probably gauche to bring him a gift from her affair; although, as mentioned, she often considered *him* the affair.)

Joan poured a small drop of absinthe, without any of the attendant ceremony – even though that was the part she liked – and took a sip before lifting the rock that propped open the window and using it to bash a nail into the wall. She slung Nina's acrobats onto the wall, and tucked into the cheap frame a scrap of paper on which Epstein had sketched a wineglass for her at the Grafton one night. Her art collection.

Nina had laughingly referred to the acrobats as a self-portrait. Joan knew better. It was of her.

She straightened her dress in the mirror, tapped the pistol in her pocket reassuringly, and passed through the hallway and into the Chelsea night.

***

I bought the gun impulsively. It was the summer of 2023 and I was researching 20th-century utopian communities; an internet search for certain symbols related to these communities returned a hit for a small pistol for sale, and its photograph called to me. So beautiful, and such a wonderfully stupid purchase. It's a collector's thing, and I'm not a collector.

The owner had been an Oxford don or something and it had sat in his desk for a generation, accumulating junk around it, and the guy's son shoved it all into a box at once, included in the sale of the revolver. Archaeological layers of desktop garbage had been swept into the small box in their Oxfordshire home until it was full, then shipped to the unsuspecting Yank who'd bought it.

Two things stood out to me, besides the pistol: A signed postcard photograph of an actress named 'Mona Limerick', and a century-old London map complete with the owner's annotations. I didn't know anything about Mona Limerick, but the woman in the photograph was compelling – beautiful and serious and knowing.

Just like the gun. A small pistol with mother-of-pearl inlay sketched with an Arts and Crafts sunburst, the contradiction of the Utopian dream and a machine made to kill – contradiction; poetry; what's the difference. Compelling wasn't really the word for the gun. Arousing. I hate guns. Yet, almost instantly, all I wanted in life was to know everything about this pistol: who owned it, and why they'd needed a gun in London in 1912; did it have something to do with this actress, or the person the card was signed to – 'Ione'? I wanted to do nothing else and go nowhere without it. My research disintegrated – a friend asked me 'how goes the Utopians?' and I raised an eyebrow. 'What do you mean?'

An old map is a fractious thing – a tease of streets beneath your streets (*Sous les pavés, les pavés!*) – which offers a terrible promise: That walking in the right way, following these lines on this page, might lead you to a glimpse of the people and places it recalls. Even worse, sometimes it does. On rare occasions, enhanced by sleeplessness, romance or pills, one might make that final leap between the streets at your feet and the streets in your hand. Flappers and Rippers, Beaker People and Saxon shores. It's only a very vague chance, but mine is a gambler's addiction.

Within a week of the box's arrival, I had cracked open the glass casing and slipped the pistol — long deactivated, I was only slightly saddened to discover — into the baggy pocket of my shorts, surprised at its lack of weight; lack of presence. One could easily forget it was there, outside of anger or fear, and it seemed impossible that anyone would notice it. I'd filled a backpack with the postcard and the map and was on a train to Liverpool Street to visit the cryptic Xs and notes pencilled onto it so long ago.

***

Nina had sent Joan a card earlier in the day: *pick you up for the Cave*. Joan's long black hair was falling loose, barely reined in by her hat, but no one would look at that considering her scandalous dress and the frothy, knowing smile that came from secretly carrying a gun. She was all shocks of red and blue fabric triangles and rectangles sewn together into an elegant tubular drape. Nina did not impress easily, but even she couldn't suppress an eyebrow when Joan climbed into the cab.

'Joan, you've outdone *myself*,' she said calmly.

Always humble, our Nina.

'They don't deserve us.'

She meant the Cave, of course. But Joan couldn't help but think she meant London.

'Everyone's glaring at me lately, because of Wilfred,' said Joan. 'If they're going to insist on taking notice, I'll make it count.'

Nina filibustered their taxi ride through London – there was an exciting exhibition coming to the Grafton, which Nina was weaselling her way into; perhaps not as an artist, but certainly as a tastemaker. And then, abruptly, through some connection made only in her fantastical mind, she moved on to the 'Lady in White' that had been spotted by a ship crossing the Atlantic in the wake of the Titanic – a spectral image of a wealthy woman in fabulous pearly-white gown who went down with the ship, spotted floating above the sea.

'If you were to drown in *that*,' said Nina, eyeing Joan's dress, 'it'd be almost worthwhile, just for the hauntings.'

But mostly they spoke of D'Annunzio and the rumour that the great Italian would be attending the evening's performance. He wouldn't, they knew that, but chewing on the rumour soaked up a few minutes of crowded Piccadilly. After a brief stop at Nina's studio for a drink of fortification – at which Joan noticed the nearly perfect yet unfinished condition of so many paintings – they walked the last few minutes of the journey to their submerged destination.

The entrance was unassuming – at least on the outside – and yet, as they passed the hat-tip of the doorman (he knew them, of course, or liked their look enough to pretend he did) and took to the steps down, down, into the ground, Joan's arms pimpled. It was still fresh, which was all she needed – a few more weeks of visits and it might be relegated to her *used-to-be's*, her mental catalogue of spaces and sights, streets and societies and people that were the absolute thrill – the reason to keep on living – until the minute they weren't.

But for now, the Cave of the Golden Calf was simply *it* and she ran a knowing thumb and forefinger around her broad hat rim to be sure it was just so; flattened her volcanic dress over what Nina had called her 'Pompeii-perfect' form and took the final steps.

('The armies Helen could launch with her face,' Nina had said of the pair before arriving, 'you and I could send with an eyebrow.')

'Good evening, Foreigner,' said Victor. It was Nina's caustically playful nickname from a vagabond youth, which had lately spread among her Chelsea friends; it would elicit a smile from her outwardly and a scowl inwardly. Joan, meanwhile, wanted it for herself – the romance of being Foreigner, rather than just the local flapper.

'Please, please, take a pew, the show will begin in an hour and we've so much catching up to do! It's been *weeks...*'

Victor had long, wild black hair and a nose that rivalled any in London and eyes that glowed only for Joan. Which was fine with Nina, who acknowledged his strange handsomeness yet was utterly disinterested in his hair, nose, eyes and, most of all, poems. But he was fabulously eccentric and had, despite the occasional banterish nickname or genuinely obscene tale, a certain basic kindness that persisted even as he spiralled into stratospheres of oddity. He was obsessed with women and men of all shapes, carnal and spiritual ecstasies alike, and his address book showed it, boasting means of contacting just about every inexplicable and must-know creature from Chelsea to Whitechapel.

Yes, of course he knew who the Ripper was, and yes he's in this black book but until proven by someone of a policing way, or cursed in the manner of which I am not yet capable, such knowledge is deemed unsafe to share.

Nina was only a few months older than the object of Victor's affections, but her worldliness suggested years – decades – by comparison, and she had known another thing upon meeting the wild-haired Poet – and Joan, too. And that thing was this: such infatuation cannot survive, and such infatuation as this, which legions of actors and authors and painters might never in their single lifetimes portray, can also not *be* survived. Passion might provoke art as its sacrifice; infatuation demanded something more. This was the rule of their world, as deemed by their king, who brought them together that night: 'pale wreckage' was the phrase Joan had repeated in the cab, and that summed them up, one and all. Floating in London's Pool.

Nina whipped a chair around fluidly and held it for Joan before the Poet could; this was their night together, boys be damned, and Joan swam into it while Teddy handed them each a drink. Teddy was a poet, too – Nina and Joan would've felt ridiculous even to consider such a fact: there were several non-poets in the Cave, but none they could name. And like Victor, Teddy was lovely and lovable. But he had something unique about him among the Cave's skinny scribes. Teddy was put together less poet than bear-baiter, a tall, broad wall of a man whose anvil fists and looming presence were enough to put off the most challenging of suitors. So, unlike most, Teddy was a poet with a *purpose*.

'Thrilled – as, I assume, are you – about the evening's entertainment?'

Teddy was also one of the Italian's great disciples, grinning from meaty ear to meaty ear at the prospect of hearing his words.

'Absolutely,' Nina replied. 'In fact, Teddy, as you're the most knowledgeable of his work and his language, I insist that you sit here with Joan and I.'

She pointed to the seat by her left, and Teddy hurriedly took it. He knew the game, knew that his role in Nina's world was to keep her from being constantly troubled by the less modest of his poet brethren. Joan took her own seat beside him and allowed space for Victor, but only Victor, to join them without contestation.

Protected from conversation by Teddy and Victor, who together could out-talk the Prussian army, Joan took to her true calling and sank into the being of the Cave.

Our aims have the simplicity of a need. That was the ethos of those who frequented the Cave, known in the press as Troggs for their Cave-dwelling behaviours. That need, the ethos goes on to say, was some modern flair for thrill through art – rather than a gin-crushed existence – to excite thought from the revellers. And Joan had to admit that this was what was often accomplished here. She wasn't sure that she *liked* loving the Cave, but love it she did.

Iron columns bore the weight of the ceiling – low enough that a man like Teddy had to duck his head slightly at all times – and were, in turn, held up by plaster caryatids with, instead of alluring women, the pagan heads of hawks and cats. The room was dark, with dim electric lights bolstered by candles flickering below the murals that adorned the walls. Troglodyte-friendly, the murals depicted further pre-Christian scenes of bull hunting, sacrificial altars, New World aesthetics and Old World occultism combined. What drew Joan the most were the colours – like her dress, the walls of the Cave were a civil war of brightness waged against the drab grey of proper society. Point in case, the stage curtain, a lascivious jungle image of rutting animals beneath crude, exotic, African skies. Or perhaps South Sea Island skies? Who among them knew which was which?

The Cave of the Golden Calf was, as the name implied, something of an altar on which these sacrifices were made – artistic ones, bodily ones, soulful ones; sacrifices of liver and spleen. There the Troggs saw dancers and actors, musicians from around Europe and around the world; it was as if Paris had come to London for a few nights each week, and the cabaret was unrivalled since its opening, just a few months earlier. And what's more, along with its novelty and expertise came – well, *everyone*. To say that everyone went to the Cave was as ridiculous as pointing out a poet – the likes of Joan or Nina could hardly think of someone they'd want to share a room with who wasn't there *that very night*.

***

I read about Mona Limerick before heading to London. An easy one to fall in love with, Mona, the dark-haired and mysterious Irish actress. Each time I stared at that postcard, and there were many such times, I thought I saw something new in it; some hint that might lead me on my chase. Even more beguiling, however, was the inscription on the card to 'Ione', which, as I discovered, partly quoted a Yeats play I'd never read, and which had the most fantastic line within it: *Grow dragonish to yourself.* The map, too, made me wild with wonder. There were a few spots marked with an X or intersections circled, but the writing set me on my course – a spot just off Regent Street. Like the gun, and Mona, it was a rabbit hole I couldn't help but dive into headfirst.

The train to Liverpool Street was interminable. And on the Elizabeth Line, a man was loudly watching a video of fat people falling on top of skinny people, like some kind of non-sexual fetish. This made it all the more difficult to slip into the past of the extremely old and odd book I'd found in a library in Cambridge. It was easy to be spooked in those libraries – visions of some unfortunate Talmudic spectre rather than a thin, uninspiring gallery catalogue from the 1920s. But this book, deep in the stacks, was just as fascinating as any veiled ancient tome. Not dusty, but as clean as the day it was printed, for it seemed it had quite literally never been read. The pages were uncut, and when I split them with my pen they revealed paper as lemony-white as if printed that morning.

There was a chapter in this book about The Cave of the Golden Calf, a forgotten, early London nightclub, and it said quite remarkable things: that the Cave, a subterranean absinthe-den and home to bizarre artistic rituals, was where the modern world began. It claimed that the First World War *started* at the Cave – or at least could've been stopped there. It claimed that the Titanic had sunk because of a misfired ritual at the Cave, some horrendous combination of a performance of *Hamlet* and a demonic summoning that cursed a wealthy patron's traveling relations rather more harshly than was expected.

That it was the most haunted space in London.

The book said that the Cave's existence, merely 18 months of theatrical fever dream, had changed the world forever. Which would've been thrilling stuff even if the Cave hadn't been marked at the centre of my map, the one from 1912.

But it was.

***

The play would start in half an hour, and Victor was still talking to Nina about Paris – about the galleries, the Seine, the clothes people wore; about him lying prone, fatal, on Baudelaire's grave while Joan read to him from *Paris Spleen*. This was him after a few glasses; his sober self would've never offered so much but rather stayed pleasantly aloof, not brooding although some might think so; more, unnoticed. No, this was the Poet with whom Joan had fallen so drastically and tragically in love; the one who danced wildly and spoke frantically and made mad plan upon mad plan – books, plays, ghosts, poems, travel, magick; above all, magick. Victor had seen and done things that Nina couldn't quite imagine – things she didn't necessarily *believe*, except that he was so sympathetic and so *certain*. His commune with Baudelaire could easily be real, considering some of the angels and ghosts he'd lunched with in the past.

Meanwhile, Joan was talking to Teddy, also about hauntings and magick, but of a different sort. Teddy's interest in the mysterious sat firmly in the realm of the so-called 'real world' – ghosts that moved things around the bedroom, rather than causing volcanic eruptions of inspiration in the soul. He dealt with it not so much with wonder, but with pure, unbridled confidence. As far as he was concerned, he was strong enough, brainy enough and simply *English* enough to outsmart the spirit plane. If Victor's magick was Swinburne, all Greek odes and 'love's lute', Teddy's was Darwin – an explicable stage in human progress.

'Not a ghost at all, of course,' Teddy laughed, finishing one of his exploits, a mercifully shortened version. 'Less dark forces than dark men doing dark deeds for dark purposes.'

Joan wanted to tell Teddy her own story. She'd been thinking about it – about Anne – almost constantly of late, given her predicament – the impossible situation in which she found herself. She was drawn to tell it tonight, as she'd told Victor in Paris, this time hopefully to Mona Limerick herself. Limerick would perform on that stage, and Joan felt kinship with her. She *knew* it was time to share the story with the right person, and perhaps Mona was just that.

She felt a kinship with these hauntings, too. Joan was no ghost, of course. But she sometimes felt like it; a shade in bright yellows and greens.

She knew the lights would be dimmed in less than an hour. But for now, she could still see the walls – those walls! She'd been to the Cave a few times, though not *every night* like the proper Troggs, and had only glimpsed the walls before the dimming of the lights on rare moments – the curtains, the murals. Excusing herself, Joan took a short tour of the space to see all that she often missed in the darkness. She wished to ignore all the people, but kept noting the leading lights of London's artists, poets and lushes; the magical people like Aleister and Arthur, and the painters and sculptors whose works she loved so dearly, who might as well be *magick* themselves. She loved the crowd but perhaps loved the sculptures more; the murals; above all, she loved the eponymous golden calf that lived in relief on the wall at the entrance to the Cave, daring visitors to go right or left, to the theatre or the bar. Made by Mr. Gill, it was perfect in its sacrificial tenderness – a Biblical idol reclaimed not as warning but as rallying cry. She loved the Calf more than one really should love an artwork – if there were a fire and she had to choose between saving, say, Teddy and the Calf, it would be a difficult cut.

'Speaking of love for an inanimate object,' Joan muttered to herself.

There, across the room, was Wilfred. She knew he'd be there. She dreaded it, too. A wisp of a man with not a hair out of place nor a thread dangling from his suit. Comparison, Nina had told her, is the death of joy. But Joan felt otherwise: that comparison was the womb of freedom. It is where a new world might gestate. Not in the longing to be like another, but in the understanding of the way in which that other saw her. She wanted no longer to be someone else's idea of a person. And certainly didn't want to be Wilfred's idea of it.

He was talking to Bunko, which was something of a relief – if her husband brought up the subject of Joan, which he was bound to do, Bunko would defend her. Wilfred was a dozen yards away at the other side of the Cave, and that gave her a few moments at least before he noticed her and aroused the bravery to confront her, so she considered her options. Aleister had taken up position on the winding route between herself and her table, and that seemed nearly as uncomfortable an encounter as Wilfred. She scanned the room for safe harbour.

There, at a front-row-centre table, Joan saw Frida

herself, the club's founder and figurehead, and with her, Arthur. Joan liked Arthur very much and admired Frida equally, despite being more than a little afraid of her. She decided on their table as an emergency defensive location – a *cheval de frise* comprising Arthur's steadfast loveliness and Frida's intimidating mien.

Joan could recall every moment of an evening talking with Arthur, memorable in part simply because he really did *listen*. He did not love her, which was a relief the likes of which she'd not expected, but he did truly *like* her. One night not long ago, at one of the Cave's first events, things were deeply dreadful for her: Wilfred, Victor, Aleister, and the shrinking space in the middle of that triangle in which she was meant to live her own life. The squeeze felt real. She had no pistol then, and looking back that was lucky. But Arthur provided her defensive location, as he would tonight.

Arthur wasn't a Londoner by birth, nor was his condition 'journalist' nor 'actor', although he was a gifted practitioner of both vocations, and the city had few proponents who could rival him at either. Arthur was much more of what the poets present would call a *flaneur*, like her own Poet – each of them despised work and, equally, those who thought it the only means to achieve honour. Arthur and Victor would rather walk and think and compose and create, much like Joan herself, the difference being that Arthur had no money and many responsibilities, which made such a life difficult to arrange. So he worked, worked, worked, but at night, on those occasions he escaped to the Cave or other such establishments, despite being as grand a face as one might see within those walls – a legend amongst Troggs – he listened and absorbed such that he could compose from what he heard.

On the night she'd first truly gotten to know him, she'd slid out of her social deathtrap and into his orbit and began, immediately, to think of herself as that special niece who carried with her the uncle's interests and therefore curried great favour. It was swiftly apparent that's how he felt, too. He'd wanted to listen to her, and that was more than she could say of almost anyone else at the time. In that first conversation, she had spoken at length about her life in London – so few of its protagonists seemed to be born and raised in the city, and Arthur loved that she was not only a Londoner but had spent her youth in the city's lesser-known rough edges, first north and then south.

'London,' he'd said by way of opening gambit, 'is a mystery in which every clue is a red herring, and for that we can be forever thankful. Too often people in this city forget its true marvels in favour of that dull expense which we're told sparkles but in fact is little more than the cocktail-party banter of the chatterings. And yet I always imagine you have truly had the taste of the city's other side. Something, perhaps, older; quieter; more secretive than the latest hem at the Café Royal?'

Joan changed the subject that night. But at the Cave, when she saw Wilfred half-rise as if to straighten his jacket while obviously scanning the room for her presence, Joan thought perhaps it wasn't Mona or

Teddy that she should share with, but Arthur, who had tugged at her story so closely before as to almost *know* where the thread was.

Joan floated through the crowd to Arthur and Frida just as the *grand dame* stood to attend to affairs of the club. Frida was an inspiration to Joan – she commanded every room she entered. She told the most famous and powerful men in London what to do and when to do it, and they asked if they could pay for her lunch while they worked. She had a strange past – her husband, a famed writer and occultist, had made her famous and given her his name. Frida had taken this token of power and turned it into an empire, if a chaotic one; in particular, she had invented the Cave.

The queen nodded at Joan as she walked away – a quick 'Darling' let Joan know Frida recognised her – and Joan took the woman's seat, filthy warm in the summer sweat, and looked to Arthur: 'I've got something I'd really like to tell you.'

***

I knew Heddon Street from Bowie – it's where the *Ziggy Stardust* album cover was shot; the view itself is largely unrecognisable today except for a simulacrum 'K. West' shingle and a blue plaque indicating *this is where it happened*. Any time of day or night there will be a Japanese tourist or a nervous-looking 6 Music Dad leaning on the wall to have his (invariably 'his') photograph taken, as though some of that alien hep might remain *in situ* and anyone holding an LP cover up could get *infected* with pure *cool*. But none of Bowie's Fab-Caesar's Breath exists today in what is called, at least by local business owners, 'Ziggy Green', with the Starman Pub and a café called Ziggy leading the charge to associate their pricey scoops with Weird and Gilly.

But how different is any of that from my own mission: descending the steps into some anonymous cocktail bar – full not of Jacob Epsteins and Nina Hamnetts but of filthy rich people in drab clothes that cost more than my mortgage, all discussing their property portfolios – in order to plumb the air for century-faded Bohemian glory? As though the smoothed walls of a dull cellar might produce smoke in the shape of Augustus John or Aleister Crowley beside a £14 glass of absinthe?

The West End chorus girls who were brought to this Cave to be artistically wowed out of their leg-hobbling dresses earned £1 each week for their walk-on-and-a-song at the Aldwych or Drury Lane – a fortune to some, but imagine if their ghosts discovering me shelling out three months of *their* wages on a single glass of relatively weak Green

Faery? I walk these old maps looking for some sign of our forebears but when I can think clearly, free of the romance of it all, it's easy to recognise that such a sign would often be two fingers straight up.

'Sorry to disturb your deepest thoughts, but will sir be pleased to enjoy another cocktail?' the Jack Sparrow-bearded, yuppie-hipster mixologist said to me.

Did he fuck.

'Thank *you*,' he said in that way only the English can, which is taken, without the slightest doubt, to mean 'fuck off'.

I touched the mother-of-pearl revolver in the pocket of my fantastically uncool camo-cargo shorts and imagined holding it to this mustachioed motherfucker's head while demanding more absinthe – Crowley or John might appreciate that slightly more; the chorus girls would roll their eyes hard, having seen it all before. But at least I'd surprise the living shit out of him.

'Sorry, but could I have the same again, please,' I said, instead, with a smile that indicated, 'thank *you*'.

***

The show was already late to start and there was no sign of activity – not that anyone cared. The Cave was about Troggs, about *dwelling*, not about rushing into things.

Arthur, meanwhile, wore a child-like grin. It was as though he knew this story existed – he did, in his own way – and felt vindicated in waiting for it to be willingly told. He folded his hands and leaned forward to hear over the din of the Cave. Joan knew she would still need to meet Mona Limerick but imagined she would discover a different reason; something else she needed to tell or be told in that encounter. This was right, Arthur was right, and she began to speak.

'Growing up in the city is a dusky affair,' she began. 'The colours are different. We have shades of grey, and shades of rain, and they make one wish to ruffle feathers constantly, but the consequences are more dire – we must get along with our neighbours because there isn't far to run before the wall.

'You think of me as a Londoner, but as a child, no one else did. They call Nina "Foreigner" as a joke, but it's me who deserves it: neither of my parents was born in England, and we moved almost every year, so my sisters and I were always being introduced to new so-called friends. Rather than feign closeness to other children we stuck together or, as often, struck out on our own, but almost never spent time with those outside our home.

'Nearly ten years ago, only a girl really, I made one of those trips – a journey past the end of the houses to the railway tracks, intending to follow the river north and out of London. I'd only rarely been out of the city yet had also only rarely been *in* to the City proper. And while I'd lived in that house for what seemed forever, looking back it was in truth about one year, even if that was longer than I'd lived in one place before.

'But I doubt I even realised I had such a limited repertoire. That's how it is as a child, isn't it? Your boundaries are the ones you see in daily life – the railway tracks you're told not to cross and the park you're told not to go beyond. Occasionally we'd go to the City proper, where my father had an office, but it was always made to feel dangerous to be there unsupervised. Even in London, where breaking boundaries is practically a religion, I just lived in my own little loop.

'Something I certainly *didn't* realise was that the river, my river near to my house, had been dug into the earth by the hands of men. I had decided to forego the railways, houses, shops and drinking dens to find something wholly natural – to disregard the city for a day and, perhaps, forever; I had it in mind to walk and walk and to not return. And to me, the river, at the end of the warren of streets we lived and played in, was the one wholly natural thing in sight. At least that's how I thought it to be.

'So I walked to the banks of the river and followed its course north, soon losing sight of monuments I recognised and of the river itself as it twisted and turned above and below the earth. My excitement was uncontainable, even if occasionally cheapened by a monotony of railway lines and houses – but *these* were railway lines and houses I'd not seen before and thus were thrilling.

'I saw many people – it was morning and the streets were full. But no one looked at me, nonetheless spoke, until I'd left the streets and the riverside path took me near a new hospital building amid farmland and humming brooks. I thought it lovely they'd built a hospital out there in the countryside, so that patients could look out over the fields as they recovered; it didn't occur to me at the time that their distance from the city wasn't for their benefit, but our safety.

'I had passed the end of anything I thought could be called London, and I chewed on the fresh air and danced to the buzz of insects. I thought I'd walked to Wales, not Palmers Green, a child alone in the wildest of wilds.

'But I was *not* alone. Curiously, from the side of the brook, an incredibly well-dressed woman hovered into my view, walking towards me. It must've been a country gentlewoman in my estimation, wife of a great landowner, for her dress was of such pure white and such expert make, and fancifully embroidered with colourful flowers, a gorgeous marigold at its heart. She had long black hair, so blue-black as to seem full of brightness falling over the white of her dress. I thought at the time she was very adult, a wife many years, but when I picture her today I know she must've been about the age I am now – almost a girl, still, really.

'She approached me with a smile. "Dear girl, are

you lost?", she said. I was already quite bold and pushed my face forward on a lengthened neck to show I feared no one. No, I told her, not lost – I've run away from London to live in the wilderness. And she laughed a little laugh, walked to the banks and sat in the wet grass in her finery, patting the spot beside her. "Come, sit with me for a moment while I ascertain your situation of mind – it would do me much good to know that you are safe and not fleeing some terror."

'I did as she said, which was not necessarily my way – to do as I was told – but it seemed in my own best interests; it simply *felt* important to speak to her. She told me her name was Anne – Anne Bradley – and asked me my own, so I told her. "Lovely Joan," she said, "why do you want to leave London?"

'I told her that it was a false place, house after house stuffed with men who smelled of smoke and drink, and full of trains and machines, and that these things were all falsehoods; that I wanted the truth of the wild fields and the wild brooks and here they were, and that it felt like home already barely hours into my tenure. And that I wanted to be part of the river and to know the earth and weeds of the riverside like my own hands.

'But Anne's eyebrows cinched together in a look I knew from my mother, whose face could never hide a thought. "Oh, Joan. Though we've just met I know you well, as you remind me of myself so dearly. I, too, wanted to flee London, where I had always lived, and as a girl tried many times. But no matter how far I walked, no matter how many streets I passed and how they might taper from highway to byway to street and footpath too, I seemed always to be in London. For London never ends. The same for you – here, in the field, between the river and the brook, you are in London; more of London lies ahead to the north, and in each direction east and west."

'As she spoke, I examined her face for the first time – her watery eyes and white skin, so soft, everything of her was so soft yet without the glow of the well-to-do lady, even on such a bright morning. The blue-black of that hair shone more than her white, white skin, which reflected more than it radiated. "You are of London just as I am, and you will be here always. This is not a curse but a blessing, for London *is* the wilderness you seek – in its streets and below them; on its rooftops and in its nightly howls and bawdy smells. You must not leave London, and you must learn to love it the way I have over all these years. For London changes, always, and yet you, like me, will not."

'And with this she rose to her feet, now wet with brook-side dew, and lifted me up, too, my tiny frame easily lifted by even a modestly sized woman. Her hands, so dewy, held mine, before dipping into the small of her dress and producing a wax-sealed note, which she pressed into my hands.

'"I wrote this for my father some time back, but now I want you to keep it. Take it as a reminder that you must remain forever London, for this city needs you like it needs me. And keep it as a reminder of me, for the day that we meet again."

'And with that, Anne slipped back down to the lower path and rapidly out of sight in the watery haze.'

Arthur considered this tale with wide-open eyes and hardly moved during the telling. She knew now it would be *his* story, the one to tell him, the one that would practically capture him. It wasn't that she wanted Arthur to love her. She wanted him to *believe* her.

He waited long seconds before speaking and surprised her when he did.

'The marigolds on Anne's dress, are you sure you remember that correctly? You were young, and it's been a decade, and it seems a peculiar specific to recall.'

'Arthur,' she lifted her drink and sat back. 'I can see her today more clearly than I can see you through this cavern's fug. And you're avoiding the *real* question; the one you're bursting to ask but too patient to come out with.

'Just ask it: ask me what the paper said.'

Joan had long kept Anne's note hidden in a small box she'd received from her mother to hold her 'jewels' – rings and necklaces she collected; homemade baubles from her parents' friends when they stopped at Christmas. Years ago, when she'd moved south of the Thames, the whole box had gone missing along with a few other small items that must have seemed valuable to the reprobates hired to transport their things; or perhaps to one of the boarders that filled out the huge Brixton home they'd arrived into (and whose shillings filled out the family's coffers). She couldn't remember ever seeing it after the move from Hornsey.

But she knew the words by heart and still felt a jolt of terror even just recounting its contents to Arthur in the Cave, miles and years away from the last time she held that parchment. A letter, sealed by a wax stamp, that Joan had hurriedly broken on her rush home that day, on which were written four lines:

This letter will make a very pretty Monument

with a Devil gilded at the Top of it,

from your drowned Daughter,

Anne Bradley.

'In the envelope, with the letter, were four coins, shillings, each imprinted *Georgius II Dei Gratia* and the year 1735.'

'A Devil gilded at the top,' said Arthur. 'Not words to be written, nor spoken, lightly. And you believe, I suppose from the way you tell me – and, of course, the fact that it's *me* you might tell – that this Anne Bradley was not of this world?'

Joan nodded her head. If there was a world Arthur knew better even than that of the Cave with its illicit artworks and fantastical stylings, it was that of the shade.

'And, Arthur, there is one other thing Anne said to me, as she walked away, which I have rarely thought of for it shivers me so,' Joan's voice quiet enough to be almost lost in the raucous din of the Cave. 'She whispered as she backed away from me before turning, "find me, when you must, at the Sir Hugh Myddelton's Head."'

Arthur was smitten with Joan's tale. Theirs was a conversation inside a tent of wonder, so intense was their attention on each other.

'I know the Sir Hugh, a pub,' Arthur eventually said. 'In Islington, but an Islington that was, once, riverbank. It hasn't existed for many years, but I know where to find it. And I would take you to it. Tonight.'

Joan wanted nothing more than such closure. As a child, she hadn't understood the meaning of Anne's final words; she'd found them consoling, knowing that someone cared enough to make her an offer of assistance. At the same time, she'd been distraught at the thought of never leaving London. But here, in the Cave, she was the Londoner – the Brixton Flapper. Even coming from the suburbs, she and Victor, of a North London persuasion, seemed anomalous in a London of Welsh and Sussex immigrants; of East Anglian farmboys and Surrey townsfolk, all crossing a bridge or two in an effort to see London as Londoners. All of them flocking to the same London in which Joan drew escape routes on a map – here, an X for 'The Cave, downstairs'; here, her studio; here, the walk along the river and out of the city.

'I don't know,' Joan said, sheepishly. 'It's so long ago, and such a strange event. And I don't want to leave here too early, as I was hoping to find a way to meet Miss Limerick?'

Arthur lit up, halfway through a sip-turned-gulp of his drink and slammed it down. 'That can absolutely be arranged,' he said and reached for a celebratory pipe. As one of the directors of the Cave, he would have no problem arranging a quick meeting after the show before the masses descended upon Mona Limerick, so that Joan could meet her idol in a brief moment's peace.

'And don't worry about leaving too early,' he laughed, curiously.

Joan took out her map, tucked into her dress with the still-sleeping pistol, and showed it to Arthur. She showed him the line beside the New River, her one-time escape route, and asked where was the Islington he spoke of. Arthur added an X near the location of Sadler's Wells and drew an arrow between that and the X marking the Cave, but said not to worry about Islington for now. She gave a small clap of joy. It was a new tic she'd just developed, this mapping, but already she could see the sartorial possibilities – a new dress revealing not figure, but cartography.

A vague plan in place to meet after Limerick's performance, Arthur stood and held Joan's hand as she rose to move through the crowd. Frida was on her meandering way back to Arthur's table, accepting maximum coos from the admirers, well-wishers and wish-they-weres as she passed. Forced in the opposite direction so as not to disturb Frida's illumination (as per Trogg custom), Joan pirouetted through the packed tables, her motley hem brushing against the table where Wilfred, Bunko and others sat. Bunko stood and gave Joan's hand a light touch and kiss, while Wilfred turned away. He would speak to her only through milquetoast outbursts or a lawyer at this point; a state of affairs that seemed more fruitful than their marriage had been.

Joan had breathed easier for a few weeks thanks to this development. Mr Haynes, her solicitor, was of great comfort. An extremely handsome man, his belief in the positive nature of divorce – and, indeed, the recklessness of maintaining a painful fidelity – were practically an aphrodisiac. Recently she had told him as matter of fact that she would rather sup on arsenic than face the shame and blame of divorce. For it was, without any doubt, she who was to blame. But neither 'shame' nor 'blame' was in Mr Haynes' vocabulary.

'Oh, Joan,' he said, eschewing the *don't even say such things* that most would offer, 'there is no law nor emotion that makes this necessary. It is abuse, plain and simple, to force someone into a life of servility to these oaths, taken for reasons so often unrelated to true dedication between two people.

'Divorce,' he concluded, 'is relief from misfortune. Not a crime.'

No more bewitching words had been spoken by a dozen poets.

Back at her own table, she managed to quickly tell Victor that she would have to go after the performance; that Arthur was introducing her to Mona Limerick, just like she'd hoped for; that she would see him and Nina both the following day.

He was a good man, Victor, with hardly an ounce of jealousy between all his bones, and he applauded her fortune.

'But you will be careful so late at night, won't you?'

She involuntarily tapped the folds in her dress and its unseen, unguessed, contents.

'I feel very safe.'

Frida walked with bombast. The Cave was hers, of this there was no doubt. Committees, directors, regulars, performers, artists and decorators would all come and go, but Frida would be there always and always had the final say. She strode onto the stage bullishly and stretched her neck long as though daring someone to cut it. And while some in the Cave may have wanted to, woe the man who might try. Her accent was bolder than her walk, veering between an Austrian peasant and the King, buttressed by the selection of hep talk, literary allusion and snippets of harsh German and cod French that acted as something of a local dialect for the Cave, her sovereign land.

From the stage she began to preach a violation of what she saw as a fragile truce between the society of art and that of commerce. What she called for was an insurrection.

'We are, some say, in a dire moment for our world,' Frida spoke, the crowd's rough music hemming and hawing down to a low murmur out of respect. Her pronouncements came in an ironically sober voice, so assured was Frida in the righteousness of her endeavours. 'Occurrences here and on the continent bring nerves to the men in the chambers, and we're meant to follow suit, worried about what might happen should their finance or power be so much as questioned.

'I say different. I say that we, too, are in a dire moment – we who reside in places such as this, our glorious Cave. Not because of the coming of new machines or the winds of war; not because of economic hardship, but because of the philistines who demand we cease our celebrations – of life, of art, of the magnitude of our modern victories!'

True believers were peppered throughout the crowd – men who imagined themselves foot soldiers in just the insurrection of which Frida spoke. Victor and Teddy were two of them. The Cave was their church and their late nights full of drink and theatre weren't mere fun, but crusades.

'They look to Macedonia and Italy and fear the *chance* that war might spread? We, you and I, are *already at* war; at war with those who malign beauty and aggrandise dull civility! Nothing, to us, could be more uncivil. This is the war for which I started the Cave as castle, and such is the salvo we launch tonight!'

Victor could not restrain himself and leapt to his feet, cigarette clenched in his teeth, pounding his hands together – as did many of the other more wholly devoted disciples. Everything about the Cave was meant to do this to people, at least to true believers like him. Joan, too, was caught up in the moment and threw her head back laughing so that her long locks flapped onto Nina's lap. Nina ran her fingers through the hair, silky black.

Frida's introduction of the great Italian, author of the night's entertainment, was just as intemperate. D'Annunzio himself was not there, as suspected, but few in attendance would've disagreed with Frida's description of *il Vate* as the 'fabricator of our dreams and desires'. Joan, 'pale wreckage' incarnate, agreed thoroughly and Victor squeezed her with emphatic thrill as the man's works were recounted onstage *ad infinitum*; when Frida spoke of the *Triumph of Death*, Teddy leaned over to he and Joan and whispered, 'Oh, uncertain winds, hear my will – crush the vessel, engulf the wreckage!', his fist clenched around Victor's. They could all quote its paragraphs like hymns.

Frida announced the beginning of the poem to be performed, 'The Dream of an Autumn Sunset', 'never before heard in English' – take a pew, indeed! And then, total silence – Joan heard the clicking of a mouse's paws on the floorboards on the other side of the walls, so quiet were the room's many-score of women and men as the curtains drew apart.

***

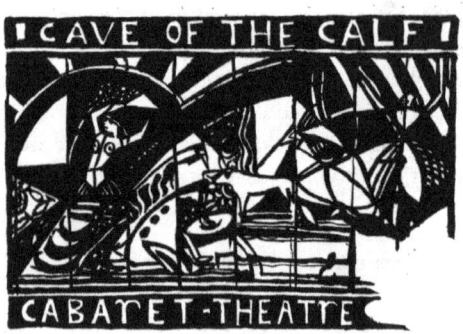

I let my palm rest on the pistol. Maybe the absinthe wasn't as modern-day weak as I'd presumed, because the room began to – not spin, not vibrate, though such words might first come to mind; *no*, I thought, *it's feeding back*. I *felt* the feedback. This kind of psychogeography lends itself to bollocks words: 'tangential', 'aura', 'liminal'. Load of crap. And yet, here I was, experiencing what I could only imagine as being *tangential auras in liminal places*. It wasn't just bollocks. It was for real. *Good god damn.*

Rapidly I became manic, wanting – needing – to talk to someone about memory-feedback, Alvin Lucier, Stone Tape Theory; I was desperate to say the words 'liminal' and 'aura' and 'haunting' over and over again. The air beneath Heddon Street swirled with dizziness, a ghostly warp as though this moment wasn't its own moment at all but some palimpsest – another word I couldn't stop myself from speaking aloud to no one; 'palimpsest!' I cried to Sparrow; it's a *liminal palimpsest* for fuck's sake! A palimpsestic revisiting of all the moments that had been in this underground room and were today and might be again. This is what happened to me in the cellar of a Heddon Street cocktail bar, in a space marked on my century-old map with an X as 'The Cave, downstairs'.

Drinking alone, drinking *absinthe* alone, is a dangerous pastime for a dreamer. It's too easy to fall deeper into the visions than is strictly necessary, with no one to speak to and nothing to grasp but a self-produced sense of boho romanticism. I began to imagine primitive scenes marching around. Cave paintings, I suppose you'd say in pun – in this case I saw a hunting party of small, Lego-sized, misshapen horses; the *idea* of a horse rather than a horse itself. They had riders flipping between skinny and fat (nothing in between) and were flying in circles around me. But these weren't two-dimensional paintings or imaginings; these were tiny, ethereal beings that I could breathe in or blow away, so airy and small were they.

I raised both hands and waved at the horse-riders. To others I appeared to be flapping at invisible mosquitos. Jack Sparrow gave an embarrassed grimace; me too, because they were gone, all breathed in or flapped away I suppose. Quicker than they'd come, the fog-visions dissipated.

***

There on the stage was Mona Limerick, the most beautiful woman Joan had ever seen, even in this strange setting and costume. She stood in a floral arch of purpling buds. Real flowers, dying and dead, populated the stage's simple set: a balcony looking out over a backdrop of a river scene, with golden horizontal light beaming in from offstage and rinsing everything with autumnal glow; everything but the balcony space the starlet occupied, half-shadowed. Limerick paced her small space, a bull ready to charge, fists clenched, in a wig of long greying hair, with lines drawn in ink onto her normally perfect face, growling – yes, *growling* – and clawing at her own skin.

A deep, male voice boomed from the back of the room, shattering more than a full minute's silence.

'The domain of a Venetian patrician, on the banks of the Brenta, left as a legacy by the last Doge to his Most Serene Widow, who lives there now as an exile. The autumn day is drawing to a close.'

After another moment's silence, without warning, Limerick, the Dogeressa herself, let loose a howl – Joan leapt slightly in her seat at the true animal nature of it all. Goosepimples, from hearing, seeing, the roar of a woman allowed to echo.

'The purple and the crocus of autumn shine extraordinarily under the oblique sun; the shadows appear almost tawny, like those of the caves where much gold is gathered. Vast, motionless, radiant clouds, like masses of pure electrum, hang over the porches of the hornbeams, over the domes of the pines, over the spires of the cypresses.

The anxious feeling of expectation seems to be widespread everywhere.'

The unseen narrator paused, enjoying the power he held over the room, and then repeated himself and continued.

'Widespread everywhere. In the silence.'

A light flickered from the back of the room and through the darkened Cave – a film projector! And there, on a previously unnoticed screen erected beside the floral arch as though the balcony were staring out at it, was Mona Limerick again, revealed here as her true, young, beautiful self: her hair magpie blue-black, her skin supple and soft, in white dress and perched at the prow of a golden gondola. There beside her ship, on the canal, a host of young, handsome men threw their gazes upon her in – frankly, to Joan – over-the-top adoration. Beautiful, yes, but is anyone *that* beautiful?

Victor, Teddy and the Troggs certainly thought so. Their fears of seeing Limerick only in her elderly matron guise were relieved by her double's arrival, even if only on film.

Joan was enthralled, by the actress, for certain, but more so by the story, or what little of it there was; more a setting with characters speaking in it, just as she liked. What there was of a story was simple:

Gradeniga, the wife of the Doge, patrician of Venice, has recently been widowed by her own hand, a scheme to make way for her affair with a handsome young man. But, Lo!, that very same young man is now seen from her balcony as one of the suitors surrounding Young Mona in the film – Panthea, an icon of youthful beauty. Fortunately, Gradeniga has one last card up her sleeve: the Maga, or sorceress, who has helped her thus far and, perhaps, can make some spell to change Gradeniga's luck before Panthea's boat has passed and taken all the young men in its wake.

All the time as older Gradeniga ('Grey Mona', as Joan's table called her) spoke with her sorceress friend, Teddy leaned over the table, giving whispered updates on what was going on right before them. Joan was more interested in the stage settings and the lonesome mandolin playing off-stage.

After some time: 'She's gearing up for some dreadful finale,' Teddy said with a hush.

Joan replied through her drink, 'Aren't we all?'

By this point in the play, Grey Mona had brought her Maga onto the stage, the sorceress played by a Baba Yaga puppet, carried and operated by a man in all black. It was a terror of a creature with sharp, fright-white hair made from bleached straw, a nose like a blighted carrot; a crone the way only hate could inspire one. Grey Mona wished to destroy her rival, Panthea ('Young Mona' in Teddy's parlance). The Maga puppet summoned a small table to be brought out on which stood a wax statuette, the vague outline of a woman. It had no identifying marks and yet every viewer knew: it was her. Too perfect a figure to be anyone but Young Mona.

Grey Mona took from the table a clutch of seven

long, sharp hatpins – the Maga pointed to the statuette's breast and, cackling with laughter, Grey Mona slowly skewered the pin into the wax. Seconds later, on the film screen, her 'young' self, Panthea, began to writhe, both hands gripping her chest as though pulling something out. Another pin, into the neck, and soon Panthea was visibly, yet silently, crying out on the screen. Each pin slid into the wax and produced an equal response on the screen, to the horror of the audience.

Joan flinched with every pin; her companions were ashen – it seemed so real, so twisted to see this woman puncture her effigy on stage and truly *feel* it in her other guise on the screen. Mona Limerick was dread itself, her ageing, evil self was despondent with amorality; her filmic youth in crescendo, pain and exhaustion present in every flicker of the projector's light. What gods were these that flung themselves into an abyss so deep that the mortals in their presence might *feel something*, despite the drink and the flesh and the utter pointlessness of their everyday dramas?

The Maga, accompanied by her attendants, approached again, but this time her servants provided not hatpins but a rag. Grey Mona wrapped it around the statuette and touched it with a lit candle, at which it erupted in flame that drew shouts from the front row of audience members – Arthur, Joan noticed, had leapt from his seat, with Frida laughing at his fear. But this flame was small, magnified only by its closeness and trueness; on the screen, something altogether more horrific took form.

Panthea began to flame – no stage trickery; she,

Mona-on-film, was certainly, truly on fire. Her visible screams grew frantic, her movements like a marionette as her arms flapped and knees buckled and soon her lover, too, was aflame, his bright-red face cracking at the strain of his cries. Unladylike, Panthea leapt into the river and yet the flames grew only higher and now the river itself was ablaze, the fire spreading from woman to man to boat to water; the landscape around them began to spark.

The audience in the Cave began to scream along with Mona the Dogeressa as her wails of anguish mirrored those of the man she loved; the one for whom she had killed. And in some kind of magick that terrified even the most dedicated occultists among them, the flames on the screen were no longer confined to it. They leapt from the film and onto the stage and Grey Mona herself, live in front of them, was ablaze; the screen, alight, the film itself in the projector spitting sparks. Mona Limerick opened her mouth to scream but all that came out was a stream of flame.

The front rows of the Cave emptied into a push of terror; Joan saw Arthur lift Frida from her seat, she laughing with liquor, and pour her into the river of fleeing folk as Mona stumbled against the onstage table, grabbed and held upright by the black-clad stage attendants, all beginning to flame, all crying out in horror. Joan threw her hands over her head as men at the tables around her shed all pretence of bravery and began to wail and flee, running in all directions at once, leaving the frail underfoot. Joan and Nina clasped hands, knowing instinctively they'd have to save one another, and each one pulled the other in a different direction such that they snapped back into their seats while most of their company floundered for evacuation from the Cave's underground tomb. Teddy threw his form over them, shielding them from the mad rush of bodies.

And Mona shouted in agony with an inhuman volume, a magical volume, that stopped the rush and the madness for one brief moment:

'*Fuoco e Sangue!*'

Fire and blood!

'*Brillano le spade! Mille spade!*'

The shining swords! A thousand swords!

Instantly the flames were gone; the light of the projector, gone; the Cave stricken with darkness more quickly than it had arisen in flame. Utter darkness, but for a single light above the stage. And utter silence, scores of guests standing or prone on the ground, all heaving the breaths they, moments ago, thought might be their last. All desperate and terrified yet silent as they looked up to see Mona Limerick return to her arch of dying flowers.

'*Fuoco e Sangue,*' she stage-whispered, and the curtain dropped.

The room remained silent for a full minute before applause began to wash over the Cave. The audience, praying for life moments before, now stood in ecstatic reverie, scattered in the aisles and near the doorways, coats and hats littering the floor where they'd been dropped in leaps and dashes.

'Bloody hell,' whispered Victor, his arm around Joan's waist to pull her to her feet; his hand on Nina's wrist, to do the same. Joan looked like a stunned doe, not shocked by fear but awed by impossibility. What had happened? Nina brushed herself off as the crowd returned to their seats, applause subsiding. She turned to Joan.

'Impressive,' Nina whispered. '*Very* impressive.'

There was an inch of smile on the left side of her mouth. This was about as high a compliment as she had ever raised in Joan's presence.

'How on *earth*,' said Joan. 'The fire – it was here, in the room; it was real! The smoke lingers!'

Nina and Victor both took this as a cue to remove cigarettes and matches from Teddy's jacket pocket. She struck a match and the ladies at the table beside them gave a brief start.

'It was,' Nina said, calmly. 'It was real indeed. Limerick, darling. I think that's how on *earth*. Limerick. She's Bernhardt and Aleister combined, but well and truly greater still than either. More magical. More of the *modern* way.'

Joan had seen impossible things before, but not so tangible; not so threatening. Not so terrifying, nor so beautiful. She thought of her father, now dead the long year, and the things he had told her as a young girl – the stories of his own father who had returned time and time again to speak to his son years after the old man's death. And she thought of Anne Bradley, her very own Lady in White, pale wreckage in the eddies. And she thought of that which she had seen in Paris, the Italians whose paintings exploded from the frame with no less fiery results than what she had just seen, if less literal; or the walls of the Cave, the Calf itself, the columns holding up the room they were in that moment. Those modern idols had been no less impossible to her than her grandfather's ghostly visits, or Anne, or even Mona Limerick exploding in flame.

She scanned the room for Arthur. Everyone was recharging their drinks and talking, feverishly, about the evening's events. Victor and Teddy could barely contain themselves, clenching their fists in victorious pose; even gigantic Aleister, surrounded by his admirers and normally as unimpressed with the actions of others as one could present, waved his hands in the air, unquestionably shouting about 'magick!' And there, front and centre, was Arthur, listening, as he always did.

Unfortunately, the figure to whom he listened, intently and unwaveringly, was Wilfred.

Wilfred appeared a shrugged man, a thin moustache covering a quavering lip, suit brushed off and buttoned tight. Wilfred's line of conversation was considered, informed and dispassionate; few even in the Cave would have such intelligent commentary on the classical allusions in D'Annunzio's poem, nor the fantastical execution by Limerick. All of this Joan knew not because she could hear him speak, but because she knew her husband well. Admired him, even felt love towards him. But was certainly not *in love with* him. The thought of such a thing frightened her more than any fire.

As the waiter brought their intermission drinks, Joan picked up hers and swigged it in one uncharacteristic gulp and then traded her empty glass for Nina's full one – 'sorry, my darling, I'm afraid I'll require this for the battle. *Brillano le spade;* it shall have to do' – and began to slide between the tables towards Arthur and Wilfred. As she approached, her gait beginning to show the effects of the cocktails, Joan straightened herself for the most difficult sentence of the day:

'Hello, Wilfred; it's lovely to see you.'

***

'You alright, mate?'

It was Jack Sparrow. He didn't actually care, obviously, he wasn't the type. Although he sure managed to sound close enough. But I wasn't fooled. I'd been reading about the Cave and knew – *just knew* – he was a philistine; I was a Trogg.

People often think that the opposite of an artist is the property-speculator capitalist for whom money *is* an artwork, the only artwork that matters and the only value by which to judge. But those guys don't care for the trappings of the artist, just as they don't care about art. The property speculators ignore this funny world that sits just beside theirs – art, artists and the entire value system of art doesn't exist in their dimension; it vibrates on a different frequency. The mad Yank at the bar flapping his arms at invisible horses didn't so much as shake the air that surrounded their melting cocktail ice. I bothered their vibes no more than a street drinker on a park bench might offend the executive offices of Goldman Sachs.

No, I thought to myself with increasing heat, it's Jack Sparrow that is the opposite of the artist. One who intrudes on the world of the eccentric but with no respect for it. (What's art without eccentricity? Commerce.) One who follows the signs of the arts, but the values of the speculator. These are the people who rat out the tiny-horse-whisperers of our London and build from their bones a society of pale wreckage. (I wrote this phrase in my notebook: 'pale wreckage'. I like it, but I'm not sure where I heard it.)

Jack couldn't see the tiny horses and that was his

shame. But then, neither could I anymore. So I sank another absinthe.

And indeed, it happened again. No horses, this time, but a bull. A dragon. And a woman. More the idea of a woman – *someone's* idea of a woman, not mine; this one was cut from rectangles and triangles and colours so bright it hurt my Faery-stained eyes. A fog of women and bulls and dragons and plants, oh my god the plants; subcontinental – not my word, the absinthe's – and women with noses so sharp they cut glass. And then a voice:

'Hey – hey, *mate*! 'Kin 'ell, are you OK?'

And now, closer, leaning over me: 'Oh! how do you know about *her*?'

Wait, I thought, that voice is real. Jack Sparrow. He was leaning over my notebook and I was breathing in his cologne, which I hated more than any other aspect of him. But what was this artless fuck talking about? How did he suddenly care about something? Thank *you*.

He once more tapped the page where I had written notes including the name Mona Limerick.

'Mona Limerick, the actress – she was very famous, about a hundred years ago. But this place, this room, was already a bar then – in fact, it was already cool.'

Already, I thought uncourteously, improperly implied it was still such today.

'And she acted in some shows here. That's so

strange that you even know who she was – I only know because I read about this place when I took the job. Are you related to her or something?'

I took out the postcard – if this fuck knew about Mona Limerick, maybe he wasn't such an artless fuck. Maybe he wasn't Artless Jack Sparrow but The Artful Fucker. Suddenly my attitude, my heavy drinking, my cargo shorts all felt ... a bit unplanned. I showed him the picture and the signature on the back and that word, 'dragonish', that started swimming around my head.

The postcard shook in my hand and spun in my eyes, even worse than the room, which was beyond unsteady and into potential-earthquake territory. I heard the Dodger speaking but not the words and then, in slow motion, the bar moved rapidly towards my face, and I was out.

***

Wilfred recoiled as if faced with a snake. He'd seen her coming but wasn't prepared for her to actually speak. Nearly all their communications since Paris had been through lawyers – and since each was able to afford a good one, that communication had proven rather passively combative.

'Ione,' he said, touching the corner of his mouth, instinctively pointing out the smears in her lipstick.

He had taken to using her *nom de guerre*, Ione, despite never having used it while she herself had done so. It's the name she was using when Victor first introduced the two of them, at which point her hand was far from Wilfred's thoughts. Not that she wasn't entrancing, young and full of thrill. But there had been little doubt of who held her heart, and whose she held. And yet, here they were, two years on, and it was Wilfred filing for divorce.

'Ione, I hope you'll respect my conversation with Arthur,' he said. 'I simply must know what he thinks of this ordeal tonight. There is a book in it, of that I'm certain, or at least one of his stories for the newspaper. Or would you rather this became *your* conversation, I suppose?'

'Wilfred, please be civilised in such grand company as Arthur's ... and Bunko's,' Joan responded as their mutual friend sauntered into the circle. Wilfred's face dropped. Bunko put an arm around his stiffened shoulders and asked the circle, boisterously, 'So, seen anything good lately?'

They laughed, as did a few of the hangers-on nearby

– Arthur always had hangers-on; people he knew and, more often, people he didn't know. 'Nothing worthy of a letter home,' said one.

'So, Ione?' Arthur inquired, stressing the new-to-him name.

Bunko interjected before Joan could do so herself.

'Joan was always Ione when we first met her,' Bunko pointed in Victor's direction across the room, 'he introduced her as, "Ione de Forest, Actress, Dancer, Artist and thoroughly, undoubtedly, Scourge of All Philistines!"'

Well past 'tipsy', Bunko had slipped into a tight North London accent out of jest and laughed off Joan and Wilfred's joint despair at this inappropriateness.

'Now she only uses it to annoy the normal folk of London, particularly her relations. And lawyers.'

'Well, *Ione de Forest*,' said Arthur. 'I said before that I would help you meet Mona Limerick, but now it simply *must be* – introducing Ione to Panthea, just like Shelley's sea nymphs in Prometheus! I shall become legend!'

He took her hand gently and lifted it, implying that Joan step onto his chair and then to the stage. The two crossed through the arch of flowers, behind the coloured layers of curtain and to the Cave's knotted complex of backrooms. Here were no murals on the walls of primeval men chasing beasts (though there was, frequently, the real thing), no flashes of purple and green; nothing but cheap unfinished wooden furniture; floors that might well be London clay. The dimly lit splendour of the Cave's bars and tables made way for a warren of almost-black tunnels, more 'cavernous' than 'Cave,' and each room populated with a handful of the unlucky performers taking to the stage for the evening's second half. Arthur dragged Joan past three Russian acrobats checking their equipment for fire damage and a pair of gypsy musicians whose instruments, unrecognisable but for strings and tuning pegs, sounded like garish yellows to Joan's ears, after the deep, lonesome purples of the mandolin set to a burning boat.

'Poor sods,' Joan commented to Arthur. 'Think they saw what we just saw? They must be ready to go home!'

They came to a door in the labyrinthine corridors, rooms, and rooms-acting-as-corridors – 'I'd never find my way back,' said Joan – and Arthur opened it without knocking, to his companion's horror. But Mona Limerick was, mercifully, pleased at the sight of Arthur and greeted him with an extended hand for his kiss.

She was beautiful once again, the lines mostly erased from her face, her wig sitting on a nearby desktop, a glass of wine beside it. She looked younger than she truly was, no older than Joan despite in truth being at least a decade her senior. Confidence radiated, the confidence of one who accepts that everything might not go to plan.

'Arthur, I haven't seen anyone without a financial stake in keeping me happy since I left the stage – you must tell me, honestly, what did people think?'

Joan stepped in front, eclipsing Arthur not with the size of her little frame, but with the angles and colours of her dress, which obscured Arthur's round-collared, vicar-grey suit. Joan and Mona were face to face.

'My only stake is in art,' said Joan. It's what Victor might've said, but she meant it and so ignored the nagging feeling. 'And in that I can categorically describe you, and this performance, and this play, and this place in which to play it, as a success; not just a success, a revelation!'

Mona cocked her head as if to straighten the colourful triangles before her and broached a smile. 'And who are you, young one with a mad seamstress and a stake in art?'

'This is the actress Ione de Forest,' said Arthur, excited to make his Shelley reference despite few getting it. 'The Ione, perhaps, to your Panthea?'

'You can call me Joan,' she laughed.

'Well, *Ione*, thank you so much for the kindest of words. I can tell from your dress that yours is an opinion I should value.'

'That's correct,' said Joan, not taking the bait. 'Funny thing is, we almost know one another. Well, not *you and I*, but my mother knew your mother in Galway. She would speak of your family when you would appear in the newspapers. When I was a child, this was.'

'I can imagine that to be true,' said Mona, smirking off the implied age-barb. 'You have the black hair, bright eyes and impertinence of an Irish actress. But I didn't know a de Forest in our town?'

'Nor did my mother know a Limerick, and yet, here we are!'

'Ahh, yes, these are the things we must do at times are they not? For our art to dominate the other aspects of our biographies – the vital crucible of our origin is one to be removed from view before we take the stage.'

'We simply must know how tonight's performance was made,' Arthur demanded, before the two women could trade any more of their banter. 'How, honestly, are you even alive?'

Mona sat slowly down before one of the mirrors. There was only her, plus Joan and Arthur, and yet there were seats for a half-dozen other actors to prepare themselves. She placed each hand outstretched as under a serving tray, indicating two seats from which her audience might appreciate her tale.

'The stage is meant to separate us,' she said. 'It's meant to say, you – out there – are "real life" while this, up here, is playing. And to do that, you must suspend all kinds of disbelief as an audience – you must agree that what I do is real, for the moment, but not real as far as all the rest of time and history exist. That is the art, is it not? To create a moment so real that it is *truth* even as we, those alive in true flesh, lie with every word we speak.

'But there is *something else* to art. Something that we can conjure if we wish, that is beyond being "real" or "not real" and is, in fact, neither. And this is what we have done tonight.'

Mona reached into her dress, the one that her older Dogeressa character had worn, a matronly frilled affair of dark greys and blacks, and produced a scrap of canvas the size of a square of four postage stamps, a dull papyrus yellow, frayed and singed at the edges, with tiny blackened holes where it had been burnt through. On it was a strange symbol, almost a letter 'T' – like the *idea* of a letter 'T' – made not from solid lines of ink, but dozens of drops of what appeared to be blood.

Joan shuddered.

'What is that?'

'He calls it the *Tragico*,' said Mona. 'It's part of the play, which cannot be performed without it. From D'Annunzio himself, a conjurer of some repute within certain circles – the ones that don't care much whether one is a poet, that is. I received it from him in Rome. An astral letter "T" burned and bled into the cloth in some certain ceremony of which I know little. *Fuoco e Sangue*.

'With this, in my performances, and in the film I made to go with them, I can resist the flames and the pain; can control the fire itself. It's no different from the camera with which we film, or the lights we flicker on the stage, or indeed a paintbox and canvas – a tool for an artist to control her environment.'

Arthur had put his face nearly into the cloth, so closely was he examining it, but Joan had become serious – as though the blood of adulthood had suddenly poured into her veins. She pierced Mona's eyes with her own and spoke without shifting gaze.

'Arthur, I must speak with Mona alone.'

Arthur hadn't heard this note in Joan's voice before; Lovely Joan, suddenly that which she'd always been – a daughter of London, with all the seriousness and power required to survive that lot.

A voice was at the door. It was Bunko, whose merriment was still on the increase and who had, from the shouted whispers he emitted, come to warn Joan that *her men* were looking for her. Bunko thought she might not want to be found, and he always looked out for her when he could. So did Arthur.

'I'll keep them out as well as I can,' Arthur said. 'And once we leave this room, we never speak of these things to others.'

'I won't be long,' said Joan. 'And then we will find Anne.'

Arthur smiled, having assumed that adventure to be off the table, and walked out shouting Bunko's given name, 'Eugene! Talk to me...'

'So, tell me,' said Mona knowingly, 'which of the roomful of would-be poets out there has brought you here? It's not Arthur; his autumn needs no additional springtime.'

'One of the better ones,' Joan said. 'He's not exactly a Swinburne, but nor is he a Kipling, which is good enough for me.'

'Do you love him, loathe him, or simply tolerate?'

'I love him, for my sins, and they are many. There are others here I loathe and a few I tolerate. Arthur, of course, is beyond tolerance or love; him I adore. But others are tolerated despite their own many sins – in one case, the sin of marrying me, more the fool. They have dreadful addictions, many of them; an addiction to reciting poetry, an addiction to me, and indeed an addiction to *reciting poetry to me*.

'But no one brought me here. I'm here *despite* them, not *due to*. I'm here because of *you* and the Italian. I need inspiration and I need advice – from you and from D'Annunzio, which you have both provided in *mille spades*.

'As for the would-be poets,' Joan continued, 'I have a solution to their addiction to recitation.'

She flipped a wrist from inside the dress and produced the pistol and Limerick, to her profession's credit, gave not a flinch.

'Ahh, darling, an actress like yourself – beautiful and dedicated – will need props such as these to clear your path and keep the minds of men on your work. You've obviously learned these lessons already.'

'Too often,' said Joan. 'But this is no prop.'

'Our business turns our world to props. Now tell

me, which of your names would *you* like me to call you?'

Joan cried indifference and spoke to her a string of sounds – Ione, Jeanne, Joan, Giovanna, Deirdre – and Mona Limerick looked on in disbelief; a woman with more names than herself was hard to come by. Joan explained that each had its purpose; those her father used, her mother, her lover, her husband.

'Whichever they call me, I'll answer to.'

'But which do you call yourself? Not always, not forever, but tonight?'

Joan circled her cheek with a finger; took her time, made the woman wait.

'Tonight, for you and for me, I am Ione.'

Mona Limerick took out a card with a photograph on it. Joan – Ione – knew that card. Not just that such a thing existed, that actresses had cards made of lush photographs to be signed for fans. She knew *this* card; this photograph. Earlier in the summer, while working the annual garden party London's actors and actresses threw for the benefit of the poor and the orphaned, Joan and her sister were delegated to work the postcard stand, selling images of their far-more-famous colleagues. This card, showing Mona with the great Ian Maclaren in *Much Ado About Nothing* as it toured the country two Christmases ago, had been a bestseller, each of its principals being considered fetching by a minimum of half the population.

Mona disappeared with the card to a small desk

in the corner and returned a moment later with an envelope she handed to Joan/Ione, took her by the shoulders and turned her around.

'This is all I can tell you of tonight. I know that you want to know *everything*. And you know that you must not.

'Go and find Arthur,' she told the younger woman. 'Tell him to get you out of here before any of those awful poets find you. And once you're out, read the instructions I've given you on that card.'

She laughed a little laugh, mostly to herself, and pushed tiny Ione out the door.

In the hallway, Arthur was – bless him! – taking it on the chin, backed into a corner by a finely swizzled Bunko who had spent recent minutes explaining Arthur's own brilliance back to him in extraordinary detail. Trapped behind him was Wilfred, arguing with Aleister about women and books; Victor could be seen approaching down the hall.

Ione slipped past and gave a 'follow me!' wave to Arthur as she slid around corners. Moments later, Arthur emerged and pointed towards a long corridor that led through backstage and into the kitchens, where the staff were too busy with intermission orders to so much as notice these finely dressed visitors rushing through their workspace.

Arthur was now anxiously holding Ione's hand, practically pulling her through the long, thin kitchen space and into another corridor where they came to a set of stairs leading down.

'The storage cellar,' he said, and urged her down the cold, stone steps, roughly hewn, as though cut out from the earth itself.

If entrance to the Cave was like joining another world, entrance to its cellar was like travelling through time. To some age not of jolly, modernist Troggs but of true cave-dwellers; as though London had never met a Roman nor erected a church spire. The pagan chill was unmoved by that Dionysian flamboyance they sought upstairs; instead it whispered of animal hides in darkened corners, and pacing predators on all sides.

And yet, of course, it was also a storage cellar, and an ample one at that. It seemed to stretch the whole of the Cave's footprint, simply a few yards underneath. And it was practically full – barrels and vats; dozens of huge, framed paintings and a variety of 'Cave of the Golden Calf' signs waiting for their turn on display; sculptures not yet positioned (or outright rejected). There was only one sizable area free of crates of drink, refuse, construction detritus and seemingly millions of works of art: right in the middle, with an oil lamp hanging overhead, one of only a few lights to be found.

Arthur lit one of the candles positioned at the bottom of the stairs and began to busy himself with the paintings and signs, a dozen different bundles of them all standing upright like books on a shelf, loosely bound with thin, dyed-black rope. He sang as he flipped through them: 'Of Sack and Canary he never doth fail / and all the year round there is brewing of ale / but ho! ho! ho! old Simon doth know / where many a flask of his best doth go...'

With Arthur thus distracted, Ione stood under the light and opened her envelope. Inside she found the card, photograph on one side and on the other, an inscription:

Miss Ione de Forest:

You and I have the cold sea's blood in us.

We have heard terrible mysterious things, magical horrors and the spells of wizards,

for we have listened to the singers of the roads.

Yourself wars on yourself.

You that does your husband's will yet fears to do it.

No more.

<u>*Grow dragonish to yourself.*</u>

Deirdre / Mona Limerick.

Ione couldn't help but speak aloud – 'Grow ... dragonish...' – as she used a finger to pull the small, singed cloth – the *Tragico* – from the envelope. This object struck her as a letter of safe conduct; permission granted to create a performance of impossible grandeur. This was a gift beyond any she might hope to command. And she knew, immediately, that she must grow more 'dragonish' than any would have ever expected.

She added the *Tragico* and the card to the pistol and map. She made her way to the stacks of paintings where Arthur had obviously found what he sought as he grinned at her like a schoolboy and waved a hand over a portrait. A rough one, not well executed, of a man in bygone dress, his hair careening at the sides and short at the front, his shoulders and chest present but the rest of his torso cut off. It was not painted on canvas like the others but painted on wood: it was a pub sign.

'Welcome,' he crowed, 'to the Sir Hugh Myddelton's Head.'

***

My notebook reveals little about the time I was unconscious despite being crowded with scrawl. No, not *un*conscious – *other*conscious, I've got to say. It is a mad jumble of words, letters, numbers and symbols. According to the Artful One, for he is, it turns out, quite a *dude*, it appeared to all that I nodded onto the bar momentarily and then was back up, talking and, more than anything, frantically writing.

Here is what it says:

> *Pale wreckage of sorts swirling made in*
> *the year I haven't got that anymore gilded*
> *things like gilded devils gilded with pearls*
> *handles and pearls of wisdom and pearls*
> *before swine and pearly gates and pearls in*
> *the beds and gilded like pearls of 5-Methoxy-*
> *N,N-Dimethyltryptamine: (5-MeO-DMT)*
> *like degrees of separation con gli occhi onesti*
> *e tardi like joan and jeanne and ione and*
> *forrest and time machines blacked out and*
> *the bird and the bees and the pale Italian*
> *titanic wreckage caseemeer funk at the pole of*
> *the south pole of the polepoem:*

> *Doetc scoe*
> *Here with our pharmas*
> *And our ceuters,*
> *optcar optcoe*
> *like ione down below,*
> *Ione de Forest optcoe,*
> *Down below, down below.*

Pale wreckage.

Optcar and optcoe.

Fucked if I know. And I'm the one who wrote it down.

A few things refer to 1912. And I found something about Ione de Forest, a minor character in the somewhat overwrought Aleister Crowley saga. She came to a sticky end. The Ione of the card? It seemed impossible not to be.

***

Frida, Arthur explained, was the consummate collector – hoarder, more like it – and bought everything she could of magical London in the runup to opening the Cave; some of it of genuine provenance, some of it, less so.

'One of her many obsessions is the rivers of London,' he said, 'all its real and visible as well as its underground, lost, forgotten or mythological rivers; the Thames, the Fleet, the Tyburn, the Walbrook, Lea and Beck. The New River – your river – particularly amused her, as she became convinced it had been built by Myddelton, its engineer, to complete an occult circuit, connecting the rivers and making them sing at some ethereal hum. She bought everything she could, including what she's been told are the sign and floorboards of the original riverside pub named after him!'

Arthur stood with his hand still held in bravado presentation – *ta-da!* – beside the pub sign. He grinned and spoke in a conspiratorial low volume.

'So here we are, just as Anne requested! Now what are we meant to do?'

Ione was startled. Arthur was nearly her father's age and wiser than he'd been by far; as versed in the darker arts, she would attest, as Aleister; as bold as Nina. Why would *he* ask *her*?

There was a long silence. And then:

'I don't have the slightest idea,' Ione replied, incredulous; angry. 'Why don't *you* know? You know this cavern; you know these ways. Shouldn't we draw some symbols on the floor? Drink some blood while slurring in some long-dead tongue?'

'Yes, yes,' Arthur said, turning red. 'Of course, of course, we must *invoke* her – Anne's not just sitting around waiting for us. We must summon her.'

***

Jack Sparrow told me his name was Zoltan. His *real name* was Zoltan – son of Hungarian immigrants. I forgave the beard and all; Zoltans can dress that way – they're born to it. He led me down a corridor; many, many corridors, actually; until we reached an ignored storage room at the end of the warren. It was down a further set of stairs, the cellar's cellar, and Zoltan told me that this was 'the most haunted' part of the building, and the only part that still had some of the unchanged form of the original club.

I was unhinged at this point. I've been thoroughly messed up many times in my life, but this was different; 'unhinged' is the only word that really covers the territory: not 'blathered' or 'high' or merely 'intoxicated', but genuinely *mad* with something beyond those.

Zoltan told me to be really quiet, but that no one came in here but once or twice a month, so I'd be OK to poke around for a half-hour while he went back to see to the bankers. Alone, with dim lighting – half the cavernous space was barely illuminated at all – I couldn't see much that could've been around more than 50 years, nonetheless twice that. Maybe the floorboards, scuffed to hell and with a huge empty patch ripped up in the centre.

The hum in my head was pounding now – a hum that started once I woke up from my *other*consciousness moment – and I felt deeply *liminal*; seriously, I was in the forgotten basement of a forgotten basement, utterly alone in silence despite sitting beneath one of the busiest parts of London. If ever I had the right to use that word, this was it.

I took out the gun and the map and the card and placed them on top of a stack of old, empty picture frames; probably from a 1970s incarnation of this bar, from the appearance of the other paintings stacked in corners. Someone wasn't interested in throwing things away. The gun and the map and the card – these things were still my clues, but this is where they'd brought me. To this cellar, and to Ione.

But sitting there, I didn't know about Ione yet. Hadn't researched my own unhinged writings. Didn't know the few tantalising tidbits of knowledge that still exist around her short life. All I knew was that I had the card and the gun and the map, and that I could hear the hum getting louder and louder; I couldn't think or move, just sat on the floor of that cellar in the near-dark, my totems lying beside me, and I curling into a fetal ball, further and further, and the hum and the words — Optcar and optcoe; down below — over and over and nothing managed to overcome the hum and those words, which blended together into a single sound.

And *bang*. So loud. Like a gunshot, but certainly not mine. Just one. *Bang*.

***

Arthur waved Ione closer and the two began to extend the central clearing, pushing heavy barrels and moving painting after painting until there was enough room for the two of them to move around unobstructed, at least for a few yards. Arthur stood straight, with the pub sign placed upright before him, and closed his eyes, muttering a series of words Ione had heard before from Aleister's chums, though she had never cared enough to commit them to memory: near enough to *Gayburrah* and *Layohluum* and others less humourous to her ears.

Arthur waved his hands in the air in the manner of a five-pointed star; there had been times in her short life amongst these poets and madmen that such actions had set her ablaze. Once, two of her companions created a ritual with daggers and blood and such closeness; such haunting closeness in whispered words and drawn symbols and all of these actions, decreed by ancient lore, which they knew so intimately, despite the language's utter strangeness to her own Brixton ears.

She had gasped at the eroticism of it all. The drugs had helped. But they weren't entirely to blame. It was thrilling.

Now it was her with the dagger and the blood, if merely implied within the *Tragico*. But no closeness. She was alone, Arthur in what might well be a different dimension to her. She slipped the cloth out of her pocket and moved to the furthest corners of the cellar as Arthur's incantations became more repetitive, increasing in volume, in conviction, as his voice lowered into a stage-bellow.

He was consumed with the ritual. She, with doubt.

As she moved away from the centre, through the maze of boxes and crates, the thoughts overwhelmed her: this was not some node on an occult river-network. This was not a pub. None of this was as Anne had told her. She'd known this ghost for half her life; Arthur for half an evening, yet here she was, following his lead as though this charade was the map to her final escape. He'd expected her to know what to do, and she had known; she just didn't want to admit it.

'Ah-DOH-nie!' Arthur seemed to be shouting now, having turned the opposite direction to Ione. 'Ahh-Glah!' He continually cleared his throat and coughed a few times. 'About me flames the pentagram!'

It was far less impressive to Ione than he might've expected. She quietly slipped into the shadows and sat down on a crate – full, she imagined, of fraudulent icons of occult London. It would certainly do as her stage.

It was time to escape this. To frame herself, with a gilded devil at the top, such that none she knew would seek or find her – like Anne; a cryptic trail none could follow. She removed the tiny fragment of cloth from her pocket, the *Tragico*, and held it tightly in one hand. She placed Mona's card and her map beside her, folded neatly together, and lifted the pistol. It had so little weight, so little presence. The pearl of the handle and the beautiful little sunburst made Ione smile at this frightful thing.

Beautiful and useful, yet what a contradiction. What a poem. What a *bang*.

ALSO OUT ON FAR WEST

SONNY VINCENT……..............................Snake Pit Therapy
BRENT L. SMITH……………………….Pipe Dreams on Pico
JOSEPH MATICK…….............................The Baba Books
KURT EISENLOHR……………………….Stab the Remote
KANSAS BOWLING……..............A Cuddly Toys Companion
KANSAS BOWLING & PARKER LOVE BOWLING………..
Prewritten Letters for Your Convenience
CRAIG DYER…………Heavier Than a Death in the Family
PARKER LOVE BOWLING………………….Rhododendron, Rhododendron
JENNIFER ROBIN…………………You Only Bend Once with a Spoonful of Mercury
JOSEPH MATICK……..Cherry Wagon
RICHARD CABUT……………………….Disorderly Magic
NORMAN DOUGLAS…………Love and the Fear of Love
ELIZABETH ELLEN……………………………….Estranged
JEFFREY WENGROFSKY…………The Wolfboy of Rego Park
HAKON ADALSTEINSSON………………Our Broken Land
.A FAR WEST ANTHOLOGY……………………Pretty Obscure
LILY LADY………………………………………………….NDA
NIKOLA PEPERA…………………………Lay Down & Get Lost
JACK SKELLEY…………………………………………Myth Lab
PETER CROWLEY……………………………Down at Max's
STEVE KRAKOW…………….A Mind Blown Is A Mind Shown
ADDISON FULTON……………………………Social Animals
TONY O'NEILL………………………………Forged Prescriptions
CYNTHIA ROSS………………………………The Secret Door
ROBERT LUNDQUIST…………………………………….MASS
RICHARD CABUT……………………………….Ripped Backsides
MIKE DONOVAN………………………………List of Band Names
DANIELLE CHELOSKY…………Female Loneliness Epidemic

....

farwestpress.com

+1 (541) FAR-WEST

www.ingramcontent.com/pod-product-compliance
Lightning Source LLC
Chambersburg PA
CBHW031619240825
31556CB00003B/18